Donald Duck
Buys a House

GROLIER
BOOK CLUB EDITION

One beautiful day while Donald Duck was driving in the country, he drove past an empty old house. All of a sudden Donald stopped. A sign was nailed to the fence. Did the sign say FOR SALE?

Yes it did!

Donald backed up the car and got out.

He peered in
a window. The
house was very
old. It needed
lots of work.

But Donald could already
imagine what it would be like
to live in the house…

He would lie in his hammock
while Daisy brought out lemonade
and his nephews played in the
yard. What a life that would be!

In a flash Donald was back in
his car heading for town.

313

Donald told Huey,
Dewey, and Louie
about the house. They
all agreed that he should
buy the house right away.

"Well, boys," he said to his nephews,
"soon we can spend holidays at our
country house."

"Let's go see the house right now, Uncle Donald!" the boys exclaimed.

"Not so fast," said Donald. "I have to fix it up first. No one has lived there in a very long time."

But Donald was wrong. Somebody *was* living in the house. Two chipmunks named Chip and Dale had made a nest in a room downstairs.

The chipmunks were gathering food for the winter. Next to the house was an old tree where they had stored nuts. Now they were busy bringing the nuts into the house.

The next day Donald got up early. He gathered everything he needed to work on the house.

Then he loaded up his car and drove off.

When Donald got to the house, Chip and Dale
were climbing out a window. Donald did not
see the chipmunks, and they did not see him.

Donald got right to work. First he dragged his ladder and paint into the front hall. Then he opened up the paint can. Now he was ready to begin.

When Donald saw the chipmunks' nest he exclaimed, "Oh, boy! I have a lot of cleaning up to do before I can paint. I'll get started right away."

Donald found a
broom, a dustpan
and a basket.

He swept up the leaves and nuts
and threw them away.
He did not know he had swept
away the chipmunks' home.

Donald cleared away
the cobwebs and was
finally ready to paint.

By the time he had
finished painting all
the windows, it was
time for bed.

Donald was
very tired.

Soon after Donald fell asleep, Chip and Dale came home.

"Where did our nest go?" cried Chip. "It was here when we left!"

The chipmunks
jumped to the floor.

They knocked over a
can of yellow paint.
"Where did this stuff
come from?" asked Dale.
Suddenly they heard a
noise coming from upstairs.
"Someone is here!" said Dale.
"Let's go look!"

As they ran upstairs they knocked
over another can of paint and left
a trail of tiny footprints.
Meanwhile, the strange
noise was growing louder.

Slowly, Chip and Dale opened
the door where the loud noise
was coming from. It was Donald,
and he was snoring!

"Let's get out of here before
he wakes up!" said Dale.
And off they raced.

Chip and Dale ran back to their tree. It was filled with leaves and nuts, so they crawled inside.

"I miss the house," Dale said sadly.

"Me too," said Chip.

All night the chipmunks sat eating nuts and throwing shells and nuts onto the roof below.

"I hope that duck goes away soon so we can have our new home back," said Dale.

PING! PING! PING!
Donald woke up.
What was that noise?

Donald sat up.
Was it a ghost?
Were there robbers
in the house?

Donald hid under the covers. The sound went on and on. He did not get another bit of sleep for the rest of the night.

The next morning Donald came downstairs
tired and grumpy.

What a mess he saw!

Paint and tiny footprints were everywhere.

Donald followed the
footprints until he came
to a tree.
There sat Chip and Dale!

"Aha!" shouted
Donald. "You made
the mess and the
noise, too! I'll get
you yet!"

"I think I have
a plan," Donald
said to himself.

First he sawed a hole
in a broken floorboard.

Then he tied a long string to
an empty bag and lowered it
into the hole

Next, Donald
covered the hole
with a scarf.

Finally he took a bag of
nuts and left a trail from
the trap to the window sill.

It was not long before
Chip and Dale spotted
the nuts.

They followed the
trail of nuts to the scarf.

Then, all at once,
down they fell into
the bag!

"That mean duck set a trap!" Chip cried.

"Well, I know how to get out," said Dale.

He showed Chip how to chew through the bag.

Soon the chipmunks were free, and off they raced.

Donald soon found
the empty bag. He
was really angry!

"I will get those
chipmunks if it's the
last thing I do!" he declared.

Donald got a box.

Then he got a bell, some string and a stick. He built a bigger and better trap.

Donald sat down to wait for the chipmunks, but he was so tired, he fell fast asleep.

A little while later, the
chipmunks spotted the nuts
under the box.

"I bet it's a trap," said Dale.

"If we're careful, we
can get the nuts," said Chip.

But just as Chip
and Dale reached the box,
a porcupine came along
and scared them away.

The porcupine saw the nuts under the box
and grabbed for them.

Suddenly the stick
fell over and down came
the box.

RING! RING!
went the bell.

"Wow!" said Dale. "It really is a trap."

The bell woke
up Donald, who nea
fell out of his chair.

He ran to the box. "Oh, boy!" he
shouted happily. "Now I've got you!"

Donald lifted the box just a little. "Come out,
you miserable chipmunks!" he cried.

The porcupine leaped out of the box and
knocked Donald to the ground.
   Ouch! Donald was
pricked with quills.
   "I've had enough!"
Donald shouted.
   "I'm going home!"

Soon Donald was packed and ready to go.

Just then a car drove up.

Out stepped Daisy and Huey, Dewey, and Louie.

They were carrying sleeping bags and lots of food.

"Donald, where are you going?" asked Daisy. "We've come to visit."

"You can stay, but I am leaving," said Donald, pointing to the tree.

"Those chipmunks have been living in the house. They made a terrible mess. And they kept me up all night."

"The chipmunks were here
before you," Daisy said
to Donald.
"This was their home. Why
don't you build them another
home instead?"

"That's an idea," said Donald.
"We'll help!" said Huey, Dewey, and Louie.
The boys and Donald got tools and wood.

When Donald and his nephews finished the
house for Chip and Dale, they painted it.
"Let's put it in the tree," said Dewey.

Soon everyone was happy.
The chipmunks had a new
home and so did Donald.
His dream had come true.

"There was always enough
room around here for the
chipmunks," Daisy told
Donald. "You just had to
find room for them in
your heart."